AUTOBIOGRAPHIES

ABIR KHAN

Made with ♥ on the Notion Press Platform
www.notionpress.com

Contents

Foreword

Autobiographies is a book written by a young boy, studying in the 6th grade in Utpal Shanghvi Global School named Abir Meraj Khan. Abir is an avid reader and aspires to enter the field of medicine and become an ophthalmologist. However, he is quite interested in reading different fiction genres and has a burning desire to become a young author too. Abir, as a person is very empathetic and he felt **Autobiographies** was a perfect sub-genre to pursue his desire to become one. He wrote a couple of them when he was just eight. You will find his naïve imaginations in chapters 13,14,15 and 16. He's eleven now and has written these varied autobiographies, putting his knowledge of vocabulary, elements and empathy. Hope you enjoy reading this book and your response to it will encourage him to pen his thoughts down and give you great stories.

1

The Bond…

I was pregnant and had no place to rest. Finally, I decided to settle down in my loved milieu, the top of an air conditioning unit. I realised how savvy I was! It was just perfect to lay my eggs. A soft blue rug lay and slowly I placed my eggs over the blue bed. I felt assured that it would hold my eggs. Unfortunately, one of them toppled over and I lost one of the three unborn. Now I was terrified. The safe vibes that I had from this surrounding was not so safe. I was upset, yet had to be strong for I had a pair of responsibilities coming my way. There was a pair of shoes too lying there and I pushed the two behind it, to safety.

My daily chores where- bringing materials to build my dwelling. During the day, I wasn't worried about their warmth as the exhaust would keep my god-gifts cosy. However, at night I had to warm them up with my feathers and wings. Everything was smooth, until the owner's dog one day heard me cooing. See! Pigeons are feeble-hearted and barks can cause heart attacks to them. But I was strong only to see my babies hatching out in a few weeks.

As days passed by my wait knew no patience. The owners of the house were as ecstatic as me when they saw my eggs. I heard one of them uttering, "We are lucky to have the pigeon choose our house to give birth to her squabs."

The day dawned, when my squeakers pecked out their way through their shells. One was a boy and the other was a girl. I cried of delight. Daily I would soar far and wide and bring meals for the growing duo. The owners too, vouchsafed us some millets and water. We were content with their gestures. They too made sure that their pup wouldn't scare my angels. However, our shadows made their canine restless. Soon, there was a bond between us and the furry. I couldn't believe it! I befriended a dog!

I remember, I was on the edge. It had been a week and my little pigeons had not yet opened their eyes to see the kind world. I guess I was a very worrying parent, not realising that the faster they grow the sooner they would part ways, to explore the world. Well, that's how our lives are. We believe in freedom. Freedom from all kinds of bonds.

2

Guru Dakshina

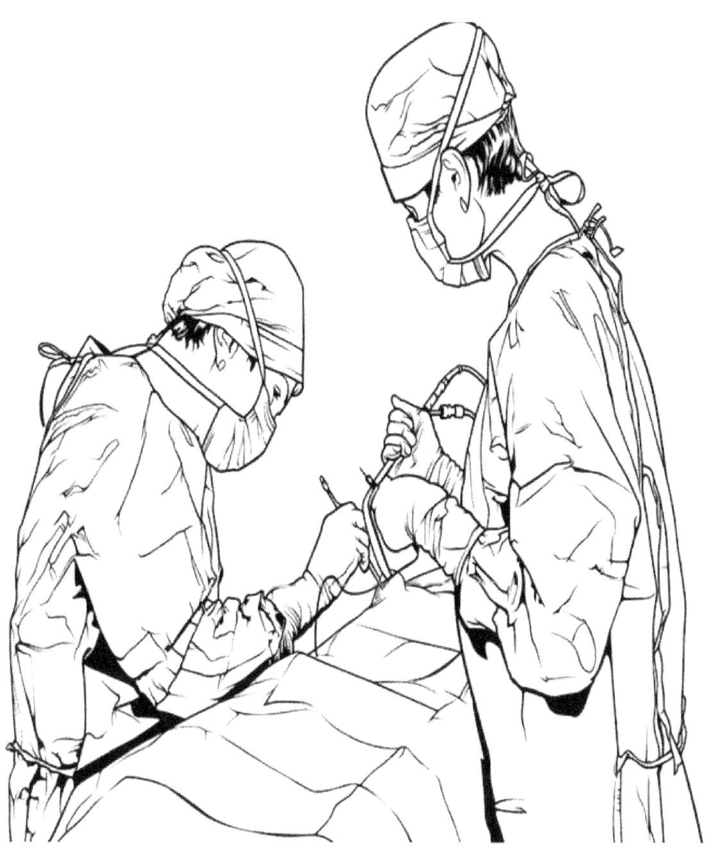

I was at a camp in Illinois and in service to the Indian community there, healing over 600 patients now. I was fervidly, savouring my métier till I derived that my rav, Dr. Shashank Gupta-CEO and seniormost neurologist, was diagnosed with brain tumour in the frontal lobe. I was the chosen one! To relieve him of the trauma he was going through since two years. **He chose me**.

I hastened to Sanjeevni, Mumbai. Grabbing his tests and reports in hand, I discovered that he was critical and the surgery was complicated. How had he survived? "I've been unfair to you Dr. Juhi and now is the time to make it right. I have some unfulfilled tasks and they keep me alive". Dr. Gupta was hell bent that I do his surgery. He introduced me to his staff as "my saviour" and that triggered a huge emotional turbulence in me. Dr. Gupta was my mentor, my guide and a father-figure. How could I take up this life-taking charge?

The surgery had to be done at the earliest. My **guru** was in pain and losing life by each passing minute. I decided to start with all the procedures the very minute so that the surgery could be taken up the next day. I had to gather myself and at the same time focus. The tumour had spread deep in. The D-day had arrived. Dr. Gupta was anesthetized. I had to start. The cranium was cut open but I was numb. My hands froze. I was unable to think. I had no sensations. I was blank- for five hours. The effect of anaesthesia would start fading any moment. I was ordered to close him up. I couldn't do any good. I had failed. Miserably.

Coming back to my senses took me a while. I dashed into my car and cried out loud enough to tear the sky. My heart shattered into a thousand pieces and there was no way out, where I could have tried to live up to my teacher's expectations- save his life.

But a few interns, who had stalked me well, had faith in my capabilities. The hospital staff had faith in Dr. Gupta's choice. They all plucked up my courage and walked me through my journey and the cause for taking up this profession. One of them, Dr. Ishaani, had also researched extensively only to give me a tag- 'A doctor with numerous options'. She somewhere opened up my mind and helped me breathe my way out. To top it all, when Dr. Shashank Gupta came back to his senses and jested "I am in the world's second best hands- First, being me". He was a strong man who could jest even in such a grave situation. "I want to live Dr. Juhi Singh and I know you won't let me die." I buckled up again to start all over, promising myself not to let go this time.

This time, waves of options were pouring in to decide on my path of surgery. My thoughts were wrestling and I was in a dilemma. A right incision would end up in a great amount of blood loss. A left one- he could go into coma. The middle one would make him blind and an occipital cut could make him lose his memory. I could not put an end to his career. It would be all on me.

After twenty-five minutes, I decided to go for a nasal endoscopy. No cuts, no risks, no tissues destroyed- only dextrous hands, that to trained by Dr. Shashank required. It was my pay off time- time for **guru dakshina**.

Just as we were done the emergency alarm howled. We started panicking. I used the defibrillator (shock-giving machine) and gave the 360-volt shock. Fortunately, his body responded. A wave of happiness spread all over. It took me exactly four hours and forty-four minutes to cut through the tumour and eradicate it completely without leaving any traces in the brain. When Dr. Gupta revived, he had something instore for me- the unfair that he wanted to make right. "I'm proud of you Dr. Singh and I request you to rejoin Sanjeevni, Mumbai as the head of the Neurology department and CEO". However, there was no one better than him, hence I had to turn him down and took a back journey to Illinois.

The news of my surgery reached Illinois before me and I was felicitated with 'The Medallion for Scientific Achievement'. Dr. Ishaani there after tagged me with a new title- 'The I'm possible'.

3

Willy Willy Wonka Willy Wonka...

“Are you one of my deceitful employees who revealed my secret recipes to my competitors?” I asked the old man who accompanied the winner of one of my golden tickets. “Certainly not, sir!” he replied shakily. “Then come along all of you to ‘The Wonka Factory’.” And I started narrating about all what I went through all these years when I shut down the factory only to return with a bang!

So here I go...

For many days, I travelled and hit the Loompaland. I keenly observed the Oompa Loompas and came up to a decision that they would be my team of workers in the chocolate factory. I walked up very confidently to the leader, learning their gestures and language to only win him over”.

I took all the children and their guardians into the first chocolate room. A fat, pig-like, greedy boy, instantly lay down on my minty grass to contaminate my chocolate river. He licked it and sucked it and gargled in it! That wasn’t allowed! In spite of giving out cries of warning he turned a deaf ear. He was sucked up by my enormous glass pipe with high suction and was thrown out of the factory... His mother yelled at me... “He’ll drown, he can’t swim!” But you know what? It served him right!

Then I led them to my invention lab, where this weirdo, a gum-chewing champion, stuck her old chewing gum in her hair. Yucks! She grabbed my three-course meal chewing gum which was yet in the pipeline and her tummy full with the tastes of tomato soup, roasted chicken, potatoes and gravy, fizzy orange and cheese crackers. I warned this haughty girl to spit the gum out before it gets to the pudding. But what a stubborn girl! She did not obey and blew up into a huge violet blueberry orb.

Now, we were left with only three children and their guardians. Out of all the children I met, Veruca Salt- the most arrogant brat. I guess she had a zoo at home-hehehehehe... All of them followed me to the nut-sorting room, where my squirrels sorted the choicest and the best quality nuts. The Oompa Loompas can’t get the nut in whole-they always break them in half. Veruca demanded a trained squirrel. When her father showed reluctance, she went down to catch hold of one of them. Off she was thrown into the garbage system by hundreds of squirrels, followed by her father. What a lovely way to punish this repellent pest.

"Do you remember your first chocolate?" asked Charlie Bucket. A lad who seemed quite different from the others. He took me years back into my childhood. I was never allowed to have one as my father- a dentist- Dr. Wilbur Wonka never permitted me to have one. How my mouth watered to have just once smack of it. He threw all my candies into the fire and slammed the door as he left. I could do anything then, as I pined a lot for their sweetness. I moved the ashes and got a glimpse of one of the unburnt piece. Scrumptious!

Next was the television room. Not just any ordinary one! From this room, when chocolates would be advertised, viewers could extend their hand into the television and have it! Mike, an obnoxious idiot, extremely curious, tried to tamper with my systems. And you know what happens when you fidget with The Wonka Factory- It throws you out. He shrunk to a miniature and was led to the stretching room along with his father.

I was happy to know my clear winner. Charlie Bucket. And do you know what did he win? He was declared the heir to 'The Wonka Factory'. I demanded him to leave his family and live with me forever. I guess I was mean. He refused. Instead we rammed into his house in the glass elevator and found six Buckets. By this I don't mean water buckets- I mean six members of the Bucket family. In fact, everything was topsy-turvy! They adopted me and we decided to live together as one family.

4

At the feet

I was born in a well-fertilized farm and my roots started to grow. Till I was growing I made new pals. I was happy and content and this was my world. Finally, I bloomed. My friends informed me about **pruning**. From that day, every dusk was a nightmare. I felt I was amputated and was parted from my kin. After all, I was just a feeble rose. Every day I was getting a step closer to my catastrophe.

The tragic day arrived. I was sent from Kolhapur to Mumbai in a huge truck, tied and pressed upon in bunches. We all were showered with sprinklers to keep up our smile and stay fresh for the task we were assigned. We were heading for a marriage ceremony in a five-star hotel. I wondered where I would be placed! In the bride's braids or in their garlands or may be to adorn the backdrop or my petals would be torn apart to shower the couple.

I was going to be a part of everyone's happiness. But very unexpectedly, while we all were unloading from the trucks a small girl stealthily pulled me out of my bunch and took me home. She handed me over to her grandmother whose birthday it was. They seemed to be living in poverty in a very gloomy and ill-lit room. "What will I do with this beautiful gesture of god. It deserves to be at the feet of our Radha Krishna." I was stunned for the moment. Could I have ever wished to be in a better place than this. I could experience as if my life was complete. This is where I could be and I, only I was chosen to be here! What better could I have asked for? When I got those pruning nightmares I thought I was the unluckiest to be born as a rose and one day I was be squashed under people's feet and thrown in the bin. But now I know, god has his own ways to keep you close to him. With all my heart I thank the little lass who brought me here, to my right place.

5

2022 Event

The finals were in Lusail Stadium and my case was open. Billions of people were staring at me. Then Argentina and France came out, as rivals, on the field. The crowd roared and chanted Messi's name. The world wanted him and he wanted me. The match began and Rabiot fouled Messi, giving Argentina a penalty. The G.O.A.T. Messi scored it. What a goal!

Personally speaking, I had spectated all the matches of the season and my personal favourite was Lionel Messi. How I was dying to be in his arms! He had burnt the midnight oil, toiling day and night to win me... The World Cup Trophy, 2022. Though Cristiano Ronaldo was working really hard to be my hero, but Morocco had different plans.

I was made of pure 24 carat gold. Moreover, I would bring pride and fame to the country, I would go to. I glistened brightly under the yellow orb and spotlights and the players yearned to own me. I wasn't an easy catch. Many had been injured and many had cried hopelessly with their defeat. One such match I had witnessed which was quite a close call- worth mentioning.

At the 36th minute, Lautaro passed the ball to Di María and Di María scored a thumping volley. Argentina fans thought that it was an easy dub. But Mbappé took it quite personally and France snapped back into the game with a goal in the 80th minute. A minute later, Enzo Fernández, did a handball giving France a penalty. Mbappé squared the game. 28 minutes later, Messi took advantage of Lloris' absent-minded defence and scored. Ten minutes later, Mbappé scored an excellent volley again. He had a hat trick now. The next minute, Camavinga longed a pass to Kolo Muani, but Martínez saved Messi during his flashbacks of 2014 and 2018. The match went to penalties and France started first.

Mbappé scored Messi then equalised. Then, Coman missed and Dybala scored. Later, Tchouaméni missed and Paredes scored. Finally, Kolo Muani scored and Montiel scored the winning penalty and I was kissed by Messi, he completed football by winning his 42nd trophy, me and surpassed Pélé as well as silenced all his haters.

I was now in my lover's arms and the world was cheering for us. I could hear a million roars and view the jealous and vexed faces of the losers. It's such a great feeling, right, when someone you love, puts his heart and soul, just to have you, isn't it!

6

Namo Namo Hey Shankara...

Everybody comes into this world for a purpose. I too must be having one. I may not be one of the most important assets of our country but I know, mountain lovers yearn to spend time in my vicinity. I am not as great as the high Himalayan ranges, yet a teeny-weeny part of it- The Shivalik. Everyone says I'm beautiful, I am the paradise on Earth. I feel elated when I listen to these appreciations but at the same time I wonder what else do I contribute to my motherland besides making her gorgeous?

Do I act as a natural barrier and protect the country I am in? Besides attracting tourists have I done anything great? Being so strong and sturdy, in front of the Himadris, I feel quite small. I may add a lot of fun to the lives of people but I want to do more! Perhaps, because I am the smallest of them all they do not have faith in me? But I am a true patriot. I don't want that my country should be attacked. I rather welcome people from different milieus and make them go gaga over India and build healthy and amiable relationships.

There have been many idioms, similes and metaphors about we mountains, like... *sleeping giants, as huge as the mountains and as determined as the mountains*, I don't fit into any of these and that's why I'm in self-doubt pretty often. I don't consider myself that great or strong. In fact, the smallest animals are solider than me. Yeah! But I don't develop animosities with anyone. Be it a mole who happily gnaws into me or the snow that envelopes me. I speak to them when I feel lonely, I shelter them. I'm, in real very mischievous- rolling them off and gliding them away. I'm actually a very stress-free soul who has a lot of pals, lot of admirers and love standing with them through their thick and thin with solidarity.

When our mother Ganga sets out on her journey to Haridwar, I, each time get the fortune to touch her feet and embrace her. I try to keep her course as gentle as possible. In the summers, so many of you, capture us in your cameras making sweet memories for us too. Your vlogs and articles are a great pleasure to listen to!

7

Give me a chance...

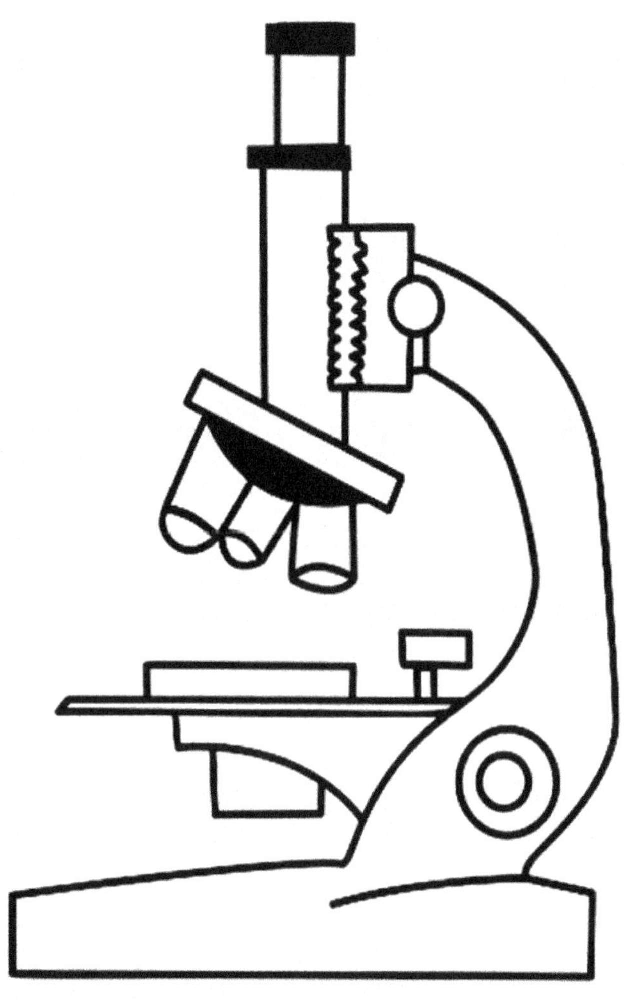

I can see through the minutest particles- both negative and positive, a prokaryote and a eukaryote, the qualities and inabilities of every living and non-living. Microbiologists and scientists are in love with me. Their life is incomplete without me. Beware of me- I can find out everything about you. Come on... I'm sure, you've guessed who am I. I am a microscope, residing in the biology laboratory of Utpal Shanghvi Global School.

I actually don't remember my life before here. All I know is, I was unboxed by a teacher called Mrs. Mansi Mehta. I opened my eyes in here arms and all I still remember her excited smile and her lit up eyes. These expressions meant a lot for me and without words told me that I was special for her. I've been living here for more than a decade. Initially, I taught students above 8th grade, but now, tiny little children, climb over sturdy stools to take a peek at the magnified specimens place on my stage. It is fun to look at these tiny little to-be scientists who talk among themselves in their squeaky voices. "I saw some rectangular shaped green cells!" "I could see something spongy". Did you see teacher placed a pink-spotted bread? Yes, we call it fungi". I enjoyed watching these specimens too. Sometimes a drop of blood and sometimes bacteria in a drop of water.

Everything was going on well but one day, the 15th of February, 2022 was declared as my dooms day by the skies. While climbing up the stool, a child was about to topple over. Her arms swung aimlessly and struck against me. I flung right into the air and had a great fall. I was totally shattered. My arm broke, my magnifying lens was in bits and pieces. The peons of the school gathered my parts and threw me in a dark, unkempt storeroom, totally ignored.

Now no one cares, no one bothers about what I'm going through. Everybody's life is as normal as ever as the very next week my replacement was placed where I use to rule. You can't imagine how it feels, helpless, in the dumps and hanging between life and death. All I want to ask is, can I not be repaired, can't life give me a second chance?

8

Mother's tales

Only two living beings can understand the value of freedom-one a bird in a cage and the other, a slave. You apply all your wits; you will never be able to overcome this sorrow. Yes, I am a slave born in the captivity of the autocrats in a village called Chattel. I was born in misery and as I grew I had no hope to be rescued. Happiness for me was the single meal that I was blessed with after the toil of the day. I was born like that, so I never knew the meaning sovereignty.

Once, as a child, while just gallivanting, I spotted a little flying creature. Mother traced me chasing it and caught me by my wrist, telling me, "One day, we shall be free, just like this butterfly, spreading our wings, soaring in the sky." I wondered what she meant. Until, one night when she dimmed the lantern and told me how freemen lived their lives. Then too, little did I understand but what I understood was they were happier, they ate something different than boiled rice, wore clean clothes and did not have to work to have a sip of water.

As I grew older, my curiosity grew with me. I started to learn more about the freemen. They went to school, they were never lashed, they were not prosecuted to enter forbidden areas. I heard these tales from mother every night and many a times with her sobs. Till I grew up to mother's height I aspired to see that side of the world.

And then, my goals in life changed. I too, wanted to have this so called freedom and I became selfish enough to think about my family and me. I reached out to my captive pals and burnt the fire in their bellies too. We all started plotting and finding ways to defeat our rulers. Then, one day we discovered a route to escape. I had endeavoured to execute it and intoxicated our captivators. We all were as cold as the dead, but, we needed to do this. For us, it was a do or die situation. My parents, pals and their parents all were waiting for the main gates to be thrown open. And yes! We did it! We all were safely out and before leaving we bolted the towering gates from outside so that we could reach out to safety before they came back to consciousness and reached out to us.

We sighed the breath of relief and freedom. We reached out to the closest city where we seeked shelter for a couple of days. We are still here and in a dilemma how to start our lives afresh. Mother's tales were true and today, we are free.

9

A Worthless Life...

I was born in a weaver's house. As compared to his other wovens, I was petite. All the others- the curtains, the sofa covers, the rugs and carpets were large. Some adored me for I was the smallest while some rebuked me and called me feckless. I was so easy to get lost in the huge piles and bundles stacked in the weaver's room. My weaver, my creator, was heard to be a very compassionate and hardworking man. He wove me with a lot of compassion. But I was a doormat. What was my purpose in life? Touching people's dirty feet and cleaning their disgusting soles? Some are born victors. They are born to be loved and treasured. They live life king-size. But what about me? I was a doormat! I was unhappy, rather felt useless and felt the pain of unworthiness. If he was so compassionate why did the weaver give me the form of a doormat? Everyone loves their creator, but I didn't have any such emotions for him. All the more he tattooed me with the word 'Tuesday'.

Then I realised that it was one of the days of the week and there were six others similar to me, tailor-made specially for a hotel. One day a famous athlete, Usain Bolt, graced the hotel with his presence. It was a Tuesday. That meant, I was to prostrate at his feet on his arrival. That moment I didn't quite mind doing it as who better than me could welcome a legend. I was quite elated until his foot landed on me. However, instantly, there was a striking, excruciating pain as if my heart was pierced with an arrow. He stepped on me with spikes puncturing me, tearing my twines and making quite a hole, though tiny. At first, it wasn't noticeable, but by the end of the day, I totally turned gloomy and was put into the huge washing machine for a wash. My wounds were left untreated and I was in acute agony. No one sympathized or even for that matter empathized with me. How briskly I was washed! With all the chemicals and alkalinity. The tatter in me grew bigger. My doomsday had arrived. The day of inspection, when the housekeeping manager, Mrs. Stubborn noticed my flaw and threw me right into the bin. My original owner, the weaver, who had been there found me in the dumps. He showed no mercy and didn't even bother to take a second look at my plight. I was shattered, heart-broken and felt more worthless than before.

Losing on all hopes from life and humanity, I've accepted my destiny lying in the dumps and I wish no one should ever go through what I underwent. A loveless, disowned life!

10

The Jab...

Hey there! I am Travis, a horse, who was once a free being, living in the veld- free to wander, swift as the wind, and vigour that could never be matched to any living being. As I've heard humans talk about me, that I belonged to one of the finest races ever found. I am jet black with a beautiful mane that flew in the air when I galloped around the meadows. A handsome stallion, who always had his nose in the air, I would never allow anyone to mount on.

One pleasant afternoon, when I was basking in the balmy grassland, a camper proning in the reeds sprang out of nowhere and I ended up missing a heartbeat. That dude missed a shot but because of terror I jumped, bellowing. Something hit me like a jab.

The next thing I only remember, was waking up with blurred vision and a splitting headache. When I woke up, I was in captivity. A man approached me with a hammer and a horseshoe. I knew what was happening but I was tied. Even though, I didn't feel the pain, my emotions and freedom were brutally murdered. I was anguished. I struggled to rescue myself but all my efforts were futile. My self-confidence shattered into a million pieces.

His treatment towards me was the worst of all, he used to lash me for no reason. My life was a living hell! Everywhere I looked, was tormenting. Why was I punished in this manner? Who was this man who took over my life completely with his autocracy? What wrong had I done to him or anyone else? I couldn't even share my feelings as I was tied alone in a dark dusty unkempt barn.

My life now is totally topsy-turvy. These days you can find me in the squatter camps of South Africa amidst filthy market places carrying heavy hauls. My master is squeezing my life out until my last breath. Someday, if you get to hear about me from someone, do come to visit me. I don't expect you to pull me out of this abyss but a merciful glance would be enough to emit humanity.

11

A Vagabond…

I was stuck on an envelope for good luck and was gifted to a birthday boy named Diaan Bahety. He was a cool kid and anybody from 10 miles away could tell he was coming for he bathed in deodorant. The envelope on which I was stuck contained a 500 rupee note. But then why wasn't I inside with it? Anyways, I lay in his wardrobe for a couple of days. Lying in there, I yet kept wondering why was I pasted on the envelope. After all, I was money, I was meant to be spent.

Then I heard a lady explaining to Diaan, "A one rupee note or a one rupee coin is considered to be auspicious", as the Hindus call it 'Shagun' in Hindi. Oh! I was an auspicious thing! That meant I was something to be treasured, though my monetary value was low, my emotional and belief value was quite high. But that meant I would have to always live in captivity and behind closed doors! That meant that I wouldn't travel places and I would not get to meet new people. Now, that's how boring my life would be?

And then, me, along with the envelope and 500 rupees, were hurled into his bag. His bag was stinky! His sweaty socks were in there even before I entered. I could feel the jerks and bumps and I was in motion. And suddenly, there was a halt. The zip opened (thank god, I was claustrophobic) and there he grabbed us to bring out the 500 rupee note. How I wished I could go as well! And then the driver demanded a rupee. Diaan pulled me out from the envelope (making it look ugly) and handed me over to the driver. My wish to travel came true. I just wanted to be a vagabond and wander aimlessly anywhere! Everywhere!

Now my new owner was a rickshaw driver. I was happy to be in his shirt pocket, trying to peek around, with many others jingling, every time he put his hand in his pocket. Though I need to admit that by the end of the day he smelt like a pig.

As days passed, I went from one hand to the other, enjoying new venues and stories adding onto my pail. But one day, a little toddler held me in her hand and ran across a busy street. A car rammed into her. She and I were all blood-smeared. We were rushed to the hospital in proximity. The people around were rushing us into the operation theatre. However, I was fine, with not a scratch on me. We were sundered and I was kept in a small plastic bag as evidence. It's been three days now that I'm living in a cold dark drawer with illusions of the girl, gushing into my mind. I hope she's fine and we meet again! Soon!

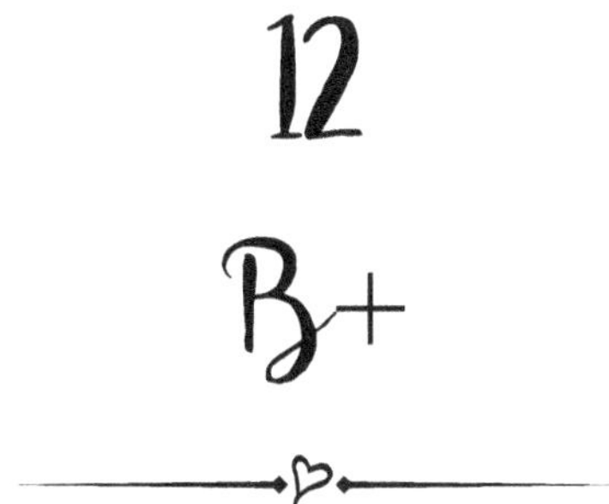
12
B+

I was given form by a sculptor named Savarkar. He was truly dextrous and I could say that because people who came to look at his statues were thoroughly mesmerized- I mean I could see it in their eyes. However, in spite of being such a great artist he did not get the recognition he deserved. He remained poverty- stricken and unhappy. All I knew that his work gave him immense pleasure and a reason to be content.

I am a Lord Krishna statue, now in someone's home. A 24-year old girl, a spinster, Radhika, got me with a lot of faith and affection wrapped in layers of newspaper, utterly conscious of not bumping into anything that came her way. The moment we entered her house, she straight took me to the kitchen and placed me on her gleaming countertop. I wondered what she was up to? She then came back with a very colourful plate in her hand. Radhika seemed to be a staunch believer in Lord Krishna and for her, my entry into her dwelling was the entry and blessing of this God. I was quite taken aback. Well, I was just a statue and a human had created me!

My thoughts were interrupted when a flow of cold milk touched my scalp, running down my entire body. Oooo! It was chilling! She had got it out of the refrigerator. She then poured an entire metal pot of water on me, wiped me with a clean towel and place me in a well-adorned place- a small, elegant, well-lit, decorated temple in the central wall of her house. She, then placed a garland of marigold around my neck, applied a red paste (teeka) on my forehead and lit an earthen lamp and an incense stick in front of me. Finally, I was relieved of the shivers after the cold bath. I felt warm and nice now. And suddenly what do I see? She prostrated before me. Why? I wanted to shout out loud and tell her, "I am not God. I am just an imaginative image of him. Stop!" And here, she was in tears, venting her sorrows, thinking that I would be able to miraculously change her life. She expressed her desires and when she was doing that I happen to look into her eyes. They were beautiful and deep. I had fallen in love with her. After all, she was Radhika. Krishna's Radhika!

Her sorrows became my sorrows and her desires became mine. She had all the faith that I would bring happiness in her life but I was helpless. All I could do was to pray to the Universe for her wellbeing, her needs and her happiness.

My question to all is, why this blind faith in inanimate objects around you? Why no faith in self? Why can't we judiciously analyse and then act and try our best. Trust me, it'll make your life worthy.

13

Betty

Hey! Astonished to see my beautiful wings.

Yes, I am a butterfly with beautiful pink wings. You find my name too long? You can call me Betty.

Do you see the tree outside the window? That's where I first came out of my cocoon. Then, I was a tiny caterpillar and could barely crawl to nibble on a leaf. As and when I grew, I would crawl from one branch to the other.

That's when I met Honey, my first friend, she's a honey bee with black & yellow stripes. But I was so sad because I could not fly like her. But one morning, to my surprise even I had wings.

I was so scared, yet I jumped off the tree to see that even I could fly. That's when I realized that I had pretty, pink wings for which I've always desired.

14

Rose

Good evening everybody!

That's me Rose. Am I not beautiful? Don't you find me very elegant?

I owe it all to my master. I must say thanks to my master, the gardener whom you just met outside. I'm sure he must be with my other friends. But trust me, I was not always like this. He has nurtured me, fed me, watered me and took extreme care of me.

But one day, a naughty boy tried to pull me off my stem. That's when he was thorned and my master saw him and ran behind him, to beat him. My master loves me and so do I. The same way you love your parents.

Hey! I forgot to tell you, that Betty visits me quite often. She's my friend too. And what about you?

15

Crownie

Hello Everybody!

I'm Crownie, the parrot.

Did you know even I was here along with Betty and Rose? No right! And that's why I'm here to surprize you.

Unlike them, I'm very naughty. I can whistle at all you beautiful girls and can sing a beautiful song for you. But this one's for Betty and Rose. "Every night in my dreams, I see you I feel you."

Of course, how can I forget my lady, who use to stay with me all the time. "Why did you break my heart, why did we did we fall in love, why did you go away... away... away..." Yes, she set me free of the cage. But I miss her a lot.

Well, before anyone of you traps me again, I'll be out of here, bye, take care.

16

Goldie

Good Evening everybody, Hi! guess. who am I?
I can swim in water.
I am golden in colour.
I breathe with my gills.

Yes! I am a gold fish and my name is Goldie. I love to swim and I think that is why God made me a fish. Did you know, that I stay in my bowl? And for me to have fun I have a toy tortoise. At first, I use to get scared of it, but later, I realized that it just removes bubbles from its mouth- standing in one place. It does not move. It does not talk.

That's my world. Would like to come & see it?

www.ingramcontent.com/pod-product-compliance
Lightning Source LLC
LaVergne TN
LVHW021145160826
845679LV00023B/2052

* 9 7 9 8 8 9 1 8 6 2 8 5 2 *